Costume and Fashion

written by Deborah Murrell
illustrated by Sue Hendra and Paul Linnet

A catalogue record for this book is available from the British Library

Published by Ladybird Books Ltd
80 Strand London WC2R 0RL
A Penguin Company

2 4 6 8 10 9 7 5 3 1
© LADYBIRD BOOKS LTD MMIX

LADYBIRD and the device of a Ladybird are trademarks of Ladybird Books Ltd

ISBN: 978-1-4093-0109-7

Printed in China

Contents

Some words appear in **bold** in this book.
Turn to the glossary to learn about them.

Why do we wear clothes?

People all over the world have worn clothes for many thousands of years. The most important reason for wearing clothes is protection from the weather. Clothes can keep a person warm in the cold and dry in the rain. They also protect skin from the sun.

People have worn animal skins to keep warm since the **Ice Age**, about 30,000 years ago. People still wear animal skins (such as leather or fur) today, although many people now choose not to kill animals for their skins, and wear other materials instead.

The type of clothes you wear can often say something about the sort of person you are.

People sometimes like to show their personalities through clothes, from designing and making their own outfits to wearing a particular colour or type of clothing.

People can also wear clothing that shows what religion they belong to. This man is wearing a *yarmulke*, a skull cap that shows he is an Orthodox Jew.

Uniforms, such as the sort children wear to school, can be easily identified and show that the people wearing them are part of a group.

7

Early costume

The ancient Greeks, Romans and Egyptians wore fairly simple clothing. In these warm countries, **tunics** or **loincloths** were often all that was needed. These were usually made of **wool** or **linen**. The Roman **toga** was mostly worn for more formal occasions.

Togas with a purple stripe showed that the person wearing them was important

tunic

toga

Ancient Egyptians used plants such as **papyrus** to make sandals. These were only worn by the rich and for special occasions.

People who lived in the colder, northern countries in Europe needed to wear layers of warmer and closer-fitting clothes.

Viking men wore woollen trousers and tunics

Both men and women wore cloaks

Viking women wore long dresses and aprons, with headscarves to cover their hair

Clothes throughout history

From the **Middle Ages** onwards, clothes became very complicated. Wearing elaborate styles and the latest fashions showed that a person was rich and powerful.

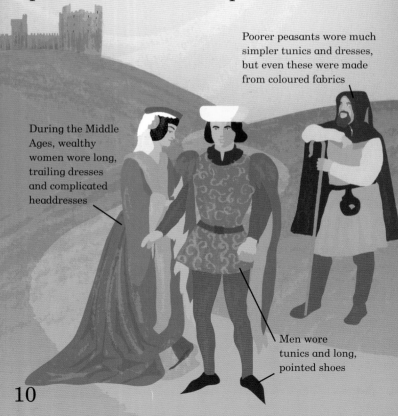

Poorer peasants wore much simpler tunics and dresses, but even these were made from coloured fabrics

During the Middle Ages, wealthy women wore long, trailing dresses and complicated headdresses

Men wore tunics and long, pointed shoes

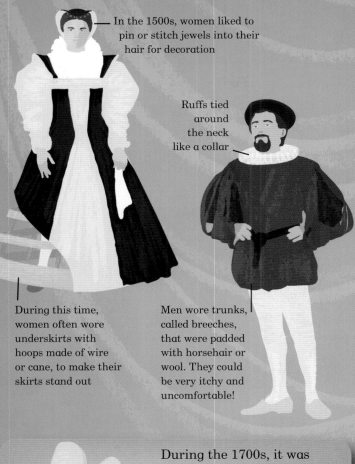

In the 1500s, women liked to pin or stitch jewels into their hair for decoration

Ruffs tied around the neck like a collar

During this time, women often wore underskirts with hoops made of wire or cane, to make their skirts stand out

Men wore trunks, called breeches, that were padded with horsehair or wool. They could be very itchy and uncomfortable!

During the 1700s, it was fashionable for both men and women to wear tall, stiff wigs over their own hair. They were usually made white with a special powder.

11

Early 20th century

Throughout the last one hundred years, clothes and fashions have changed a great deal.

During the 1900s, it was fashionable for women to wear **corsets** under their dresses that made their waists much smaller

Corsets often tied at the back and needed to be laced up tightly by a helper!

By the 1920s, the corset had been replaced by softer garments. Dresses had beads and fringes added to them and young women dancing in these outfits were known as 'flappers'

Rationing during World War Two meant that fabric and clothes were hard to come by. Both men and women wore smart, unfussy suits

After the war, a style called the 'New Look' came into fashion for women, with full skirts and fitted tops

In Britain during the 1950s, many young men liked to wear suits with long jackets and velvet collars, thin ties and narrow trousers. They were called 'teddy boys'

13

Late 20th century

The 1960s was a time of great change. Young people wanted a peaceful, happy world, and they dressed for fun.

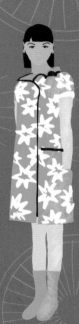

Bright colours and bold patterns were in style.

Girls wore shorter skirts than ever before, called 'minis'.

New materials, such as plastic and even paper were used to make clothes.

Hippies believed that clothes should express who you really were. They liked to wear styles from around the world, plus beads and flowing scarves.

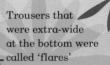

Trousers that were extra-wide at the bottom were called 'flares'

Punks often **dyed** their hair and wore it in spiky styles

Punk style began in the 1970s. Punks liked to cut holes in their clothes and wore studs and safety pins.

Platform shoes were popular in the 1970s and were worn by both men and women.

15

In the East

In many countries, people have worn the same styles of clothes for a long time. This is usually because the clothes suit the weather for that country or the kind of work that people tend to do.

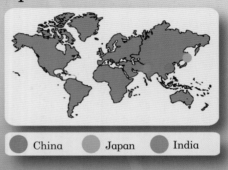

China   Japan   India

These people working in a Chinese paddy field (where rice is grown) wear a traditional hat that keeps the sun out of their eyes and helps to keep them cool.

If you have a computer,
you can download a poster of
different world costumes from
www.ladybird.com/madabout

The kimono is the national dress of Japan. The word
'kimono' originally meant 'clothing', but now it is
usually used for a full-length, T-shaped robe with wide
sleeves, worn by both men and women.

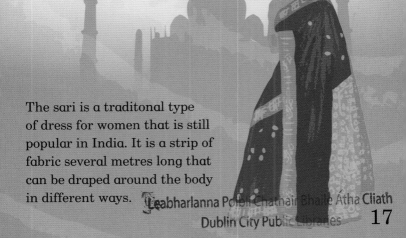

The sari is a traditonal type
of dress for women that is still
popular in India. It is a strip of
fabric several metres long that
can be draped around the body
in different ways.

17

The Western world

The Western world also has many different clothing traditions. Some of these are still in use today, either as everyday clothes or just for formal or special occasions.

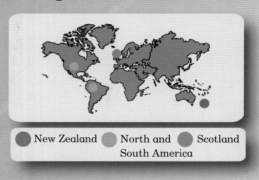

New Zealand — North and South America — Scotland

The Maori people of New Zealand wear traditional costumes for special occasions. For men, the basic outfit is a belt and a type of skirt made from the flax plant. This skirt is called a 'piupiu'.

poncho

North American cowboys and South American **gauchos** ride horses and herd cattle for a living. They wear clothing that is hard wearing and practical, such as the poncho. This is put on over the head of a gaucho to protect him from the cold nights. It is also used as a saddle blanket for riding.

The Scottish kilt was originally a long piece of clothing worn over the upper and lower body, like a cloak. Today, it refers to a pleated skirt made with a specially patterned material called tartan. Each tartan pattern relates to a particular clan, or family.

19

Hot and cold

In hot places, people either wear very little, or have invented clothes that both cover and keep them cool. In cold places, some people still wear animal skins, but today there are also many warm and comfortable modern materials.

A number of **tribes** who live in hot, damp rainforests hardly wear any clothes other than a loincloth around their hips. Instead, they decorate their bodies with colourful paints made from plants. They may also wear headdresses and jewellery made from bones and feathers.

The Bedouin people of the Middle East wear long, flowing robes that allow air to flow around their bodies to keep them cool, and also protect them from the sun.

Inuit people who live close to the North Pole traditionally wear **caribou**, seal or polar bear fur clothing.

goggles

warm hat

wind-proof jacket

thick gloves

The only people who live in the Antarctic are scientists. Their clothing has to protect them from extreme cold, and also very strong winds.

21

Uniforms

As well as showing that the wearer is part of a group, uniforms can also have a practical use, such as for protection or **camouflage**.

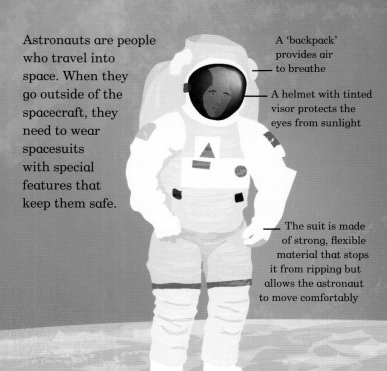

Astronauts are people who travel into space. When they go outside of the spacecraft, they need to wear spacesuits with special features that keep them safe.

A 'backpack' provides air to breathe

A helmet with tinted visor protects the eyes from sunlight

The suit is made of strong, flexible material that stops it from ripping but allows the astronaut to move comfortably

Soldiers wear different uniforms depending on where they are working. This outfit is designed to blend in with the desert background.

Surgeons and nurses wear loose clothes called 'scrubs' that are easy to keep clean, and leave their hands and arms free. They also wear masks to help prevent the spread of germs.

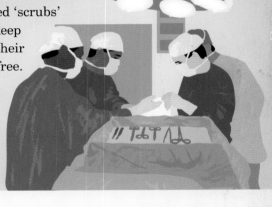

Hard hats must be worn on building sites as they protect people from falling objects. A bright, fluorescent jacket also helps people to be seen clearly.

23

Dressing up

Many people enjoy dressing up, whether in a fancy dress costume or in clothes designed for special occasions.

In a number of western countries such as Britain, America and Canada, people celebrate the festival of Halloween on 31st October by wearing fancy dress.

Costumes are traditionally of monsters – such as witches, ghosts, skeletons and vampires!

In the western world, most wedding dresses tend to be white. However, before the 1800s, both the bride and groom usually just wore their best clothes.

A modern wedding

A bride and groom from the 1500s

In many other countries, people get married in colourful, traditional clothes. This couple are dressed in traditional Indian clothes. Red is a very popular colour for Indian weddings and is thought to bring good luck.

25

Amazing accessories

Over the years, all kinds of things have been used to decorate basic costumes, such as jewellery, scarves, beads, belts and hats. Many of these are useful, but others are just for decoration.

Originally, jewellery was made from animal bones, shells and teeth, or natural stone.

Today, jewellery can be made from almost anything, from precious metals like gold and silver to sparkly jewels, and even materials like wood and plastic!

Shoes, boots and sandals protect our feet from the ground, but are often beautifully made and decorated.

Hats can be used to protect the head but have also been worn as an accessory for hundreds of years, particularly for special occasions.

Umbrellas were first used to keep off the rain in the 1700s. Parasols look like umbrellas but they are used to protect people from the heat of the sun.

27

Fabulous factfile

- In the 1800s, special collapsible hats were invented for men to take to the opera or theatre. They were squashed flat to fit under a seat and then could be sprung back into shape again.

- In the west, there are three levels of formal suits for men: morning dress, black tie and white tie, which is the most formal.

- For thousands of years, children wore the same style of fussy, formal clothes as adults. These must have been very difficult to play in! Children's clothes only began to have a style of their own from the late 1800s, and became more casual in the twentieth century.

- One of the most important fashion inventions was the sewing machine, in the 1800s. This meant clothes could be made much more quickly and cheaply. Until then, everything was sewn by hand.

- Swimsuits have changed a lot over the years. Women in the 1800s wore baggy bathing dresses that covered most of the body. They changed in a hut on wheels called a 'bathing machine' that was wheeled down to the sea so no one would see them.

- When corsets were used to hold in the waist, women sometimes wore them so tightly that they could not breathe properly, and fainted. Some women even accidentally broke their ribs!

- Many items of clothing such as gloves and shoes are made from natural rubber. This comes from the **sap** of the rubber tree and is collected by making a cut in the bark of the tree and letting the sap drip out.

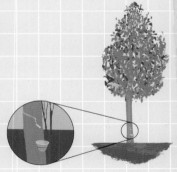

- Until about two hundred years ago, it was fashionable for young boys to wear dresses and have long, curly hair until they were about six years old.

Glossary

caribou – large reindeer found in North America.

corset – stiff, tightly fitted underwear worn by women to make the waist smaller.

camouflage – a way of hiding by blending in with the surroundings.

dyed – changed to a different colour.

gaucho – a South American cowboy.

hippies – young people, especially in the 1960s and 1970s, who believed in peace for the world.

Ice Age – a time thousands of years ago when there were many sheets of ice over the Earth's surface and it was very cold.

linen – a cloth made from the stalks of the flax plant.

loincloth – a piece of material worn around the hips.

Middle Ages – a period in the history of Europe that ran from about 476 to 1453.

papyrus – a type of plant used in ancient Egypt to make paper and shoes.

platform shoes – shoes popular in the 1970s that had a very thick sole.

rationing – a system used during and after World War Two in which people were only allowed a certain amount of food and goods.

sap – the liquid in a plant or tree.

toga – a piece of clothing made from a single strip of cloth wrapped around the body.

tribe – a group of people who share a culture.

tunic – a loose piece of clothing that looks like a simple dress.

wool – the hair from a sheep, goat or other animal, and the cloth made from it.